anythink

Robin Hill School

Class Mom

Written by Margaret McNamara
Illustrated by Mike Gordon

Ready-to-Read

Simon Spotlight
New York   London   Toronto   Sydney   New Delhi

For Natalie
—M. M.

SIMON SPOTLIGHT
An imprint of Simon & Schuster Children's Publishing Division
1230 Avenue of the Americas, New York, NY 10020
Text copyright © 2009 by Margaret McNamara
Illustrations copyright © 2009 by Mike Gordon
SIMON SPOTLIGHT and related logo and READY-TO-READ
are registered trademarks of Simon & Schuster, Inc.
Designed by Chris Grassi
The text of this book was set in Century Schoolbook.
Manufactured in the United States of America
First Aladdin Paperbacks edition June 2009
6 8 10 9 7 5
Library of Congress Cataloging-in-Publication Data
McNamara, Margaret.
Class mom / written by Margaret McNamara ;
illustrated by Mike Gordon.—1st Aladdin Paperbacks ed.
p. cm.—(Robin Hill School) (Ready-to-read)
Summary: Nia is afraid to tell her mother, who is shy because she
speaks little English, that Nia volunteered her to organize a party for
the first graders of Robin Hill School.
ISBN: 978-1-4169-5537-5
[1. Mothers and daughters—Fiction. 2. Hispanic Americans—Fiction.
3. Bilingualism—Fiction. 4. Schools—Fiction.]
I. Gordon, Mike, 1948 Mar. 16 — ill. II. Title.
PZ7.M47879343Dad 2007
[E]—dc22
2009002148
1217 LAK

Mrs. Connor's class
had worked hard all year.
"We need to have a party!"
said Mrs. Connor.

"Hooray!" said the
first graders.

"My mama will help you,"
said Nia.
"She wants to be class mom!"

But Nia's mama did not
want to be class mom.

And Nia knew it.

Nia's mom was shy.
She did not speak
much English.

She spoke Spanish.

That weekend,
Nia watched TV
with her family.

They went to church.
Then they had a big
family meal.

But Nia did not tell
her mother that
she was class mom.

The party was getting closer.
"What are your mom's plans?"
asked Mrs. Connor.

"Oh," said Nia. "You will see."
Nia felt a little sick inside.

The day of the party arrived.
Nia told her mama
she was too sick
to go to school.

Her mama did not
believe her.

Nia told her mama
that school was closed.

Her mama did not
believe her again.

Finally Nia told
her mama the truth.

"There is a party
    this morning," she said.
"And you are in charge!"

Nia's mama walked
Nia to school.
She did not say a word.

She gave Nia a kiss
and left.

Nia felt bad, bad, bad.
There would be no party.

And it would be her fault.

Then there was a
knock on the door.
It was Nia's mom!

She had cupcakes,
and drinks,
and plates,
and napkins.

She even had fruit
and rice pudding.

The party was great!

Nia's mom gave
Nia a big hug.
"Te amo," she said.
"I love you."

"You are the best class
mom ever," said Nia.

"And the best mamá, too!"